Phoebe and the Gypsy

AN
ORCA
YOUNG
READER

Phoebe and the Gypsy

ANDREA SPALDING

ORCA BOOK PUBLISHERS

Canadian Cataloguing in Publication Data
Spalding, Andrea.
Phoebe and the gypsy

ISBN 1-55143-135-1

I. Title.
PS8587.P213P56 1999   jC813'.54   C99-910038-6
PZ7.S7335Ph 1999

Library of Congress Catalog Card Number: 98-83010

Orca Book Publishers gratefully acknowledges the support of
our publishing programs provided by the following agencies:
the Department of Canadian Heritage, The Canada Council
for the Arts, and the British Columbia Arts Council.
Canadä

Cover design by Christine Toller
Cover and interior illustrations by Sheena Lott
Printed and bound in Canada

IN CANADA	IN THE UNITED STATES
Orca Book Publishers	Orca Book Publishers
PO Box 5626, Station B	PO Box 468
Victoria, BC Canada	Custer, WA USA
V8R 6S4	98240-0468

01 00 99   5   4   3   2   1

For my only granddaughter, Brandy Leanne,
and for
Janet, the Romany who inspired this story.

My mother told me, I never should,
Play with the Gypsies in the wood,
If I did, she would say,
Naughty little girl to disobey.

Traditional English rhyme

Chapter 1

CLUNK … The small chunk of slate dropped smack in the middle of the eighth square of the hopscotch game.

"Yes!" Phoebe exclaimed under her breath. Expertly she hopped across the chalked-up sidewalk, bent down on one leg to pick up the slate, and triumphantly returned to the start with barely a wobble.

She eyed the ninth square and swung her arm a couple of times to test the weight of the slate against the distance she needed.

Playing on her own wasn't fun unless she really challenged herself. Today she was determined to complete the game all in one turn.

Suddenly another sound distracted her. The slap of a skipping rope and a girl's thin high voice came drifting over the garden wall beside her.

I saw Esau sawing wood,
Esau saw I saw him.
Though Esau saw I saw him saw,
Esau went on sawing.

Phoebe giggled. She knew lots of skipping games, but she hadn't heard that one before. It must be an English one, she thought. She abandoned her hopscotch and ran along the wall until she reached the next cottage gate. She peeped over and saw a younger girl skipping along the garden path.

"Hi," called Phoebe over the gate.

The young girl paused and looked at

her. "I bet I know who you are. You're Phoebe Hiller from Canada. I know your grandma," she finished cheekily.

Phoebe felt a rush of irritation. The one thing she hated about visiting her English grandma was the fact that the whole village knew who she was, before she knew them. It was weird.

"Well, I know her better than you," she replied firmly.

"Bet you don't," argued the girl with a grin.

"'Course I do ... She's my grandma."

"Well she's not seen you for years, but she babysits me every Tuesday night." The child stuck out her tongue triumphantly and began to skip again.

Phoebe sighed. Grandma Hiller lived in a tiny English village with only a church, pub, and what Grandma called the Post Office, a tiny store selling groceries and candies as well as dealing with the mail. It was a very pretty village, but lonely. This kid was the first one she'd met.

Phoebe tried again. "What's your name?"

"Fiona. Can you do this?" Fiona speeded up her skipping until the rope was a blur and her feet made a rapid staccato on the concrete.

"Sometimes … want to play hopscotch?"

"Can't. I'm waiting for Mum. We're driving to Winchester Market."

There was a distant sound of a garage door opening. Fiona gathered up her rope and disappeared around the corner of the cottage with only a wave of her hand.

Phoebe wandered unhappily into Grandma's kitchen.

"How come everyone bugs me?" she complained.

"We don't see many strangers in this village," Grandma explained.

"It's like I'm the only show in town," cried Phoebe in frustration. "'Watch Phoebe — The Great Canadian Granddaughter — show repeats every ten minutes!'"

Grandma laughed and hugged her. "You *are* the celebrity of the moment, but don't worry, the village will soon get used to you."

Phoebe remained unconvinced. She took her book down to the end of the back garden, where she lay on the turf under the concealing boughs of a weeping willow tree and listened to the soothing chuckles of the stream.

This was her favourite place. The stream ran right through the middle of the village, with the High Street buildings backing onto its banks on one side and the cottages on Acorn Lane backing onto its other bank. Little paths and bridges wandered to and fro, linking the gardens. It was peaceful and gave her a space to think.

Phoebe wasn't really enjoying her holiday. The problem was that Grandma had lived here forever, her dad was born here, but she was born in Canada. She felt like an alien.

In England everything was different: clothes, food, money. Even the language was a different kind of English. Phoebe was supposed to know about the differences because her dad was English. She didn't. But what really freaked her out was to walk down a village street in this strange country and have a perfect stranger say, "Hello, you must be Mrs. Hiller's granddaughter. You have a look of your father, dear." It was impossible to be an anonymous kid. Phoebe felt as though all eyes were watching and judging her.

Phoebe's troubles finally came to a head the day her parents decided to visit an old friend in London.

"We won't be sightseeing, Phoebe," her father explained, "just nattering away for hours. We'll be there a couple of days. Do you want to come, or stay here?"

"Of course she'll stay," interrupted Grandma firmly. "I've invited some cronies for lunch. I'd like them to meet her."

Phoebe nodded in agreement. Both plans

sounded boring, but at Grandma's she had the freedom to explore around the village on her own. Visiting in the big city of London she would have to sit and listen all day to the adults' uninteresting chatter.

Unfortunately Phoebe didn't realize what Grandma meant by "lunch."

"My guests will be arriving soon," Grandma reminded her. "Can you run upstairs and change into a dress?"

Phoebe gazed at her in astonishment. "I'm wearing clean jeans and T-shirt … I've only packed one dress … for special occasions."

"We wear dresses when visitors are invited for lunch," said Grandma firmly.

Phoebe changed into her dress.

It was fun setting the table. Phoebe picked flowers for the little glass vase in the centre and folded the napkins into water lilies like the ones in her origami book. Then Mrs. Jones and Miss Abbots arrived in flowered dresses and Sunday best hats. Phoebe was glad she had changed.

Grandma introduced Phoebe to Mrs. Jones and Miss Abbots. They both smiled and shook her hand and everyone sat down to eat.

Phoebe stared at the food in disbelief. She had never imagined being invited to lunch, then offered sandwiches the size of a toonie. Grandma handed her a plate of the tiniest sandwiches Phoebe had ever seen. They were barely one bite each, so she took a handful.

"PHOEBE!" said Grandma in a warning tone. Phoebe looked around. Grandma and Mrs. Jones had two sandwiches on their plates and Miss Abbots only had one.

"Sorry," Phoebe muttered and tipped her plate so several fell back.

Mrs. Jones and Miss Abbots exchanged looks.

The meal went from bad to worse.

The conversation bounced among the adults about people Phoebe had never heard of, and though she nibbled like a mouse, she finished her two sandwiches long before anyone else. She reached out her hand for a third and knocked over Miss Abbots' cup of tea. There was a flurry of napkins as everyone quickly mopped up the spill.

Miss Abbots patted Phoebe's hand. "Accidents will happen," she said with a brittle laugh, but her lips pinched together when she saw the tea had splashed her dress.

Phoebe shrank back into her chair with a hard lump in her throat. She dared not reach for anything else. It was ages before Grandma realized she wasn't eating and offered her the plate of scones. To Phoebe's relief, the dishes of butter and jam were right in front of her. She picked up the spreader in the butter dish and began to butter her scone.

"Use your butter knife," whispered

Grandma, exasperated. "You're not a heathen."

Grandma's criticism was the last straw. The lump in Phoebe's throat grew too big to handle. She pushed back her chair and stood up shakily.

"No I'm not," Phoebe said in a strangled voice. "I'm Canadian and I've never heard of a butter knife." And she ran outside to the stream and wondered if she should drown herself to save further embarrassment.

That's when the holiday began to get really odd.

Chapter 2

Phoebe glared angrily at the water. She blinked rapidly, fighting back tears. The sunlight glinting on the rippling surface played tricks on her eyes. Phoebe's reflection stared back from the stream, wavered in the ripples, then seemed to change.

A white-haired elderly woman lay in the stream. The woman's eyes closed and she slipped slowly under the surface of the water and disappeared under the water weed.

A feeling of panic swept through Phoebe's body. Something like this had happened once before back home in Vancouver. Out of the blue she'd imagined seeing her friend, Jess, lying in the middle of a road crying. A day later Jess had fallen off her bike and broken her leg.

Phoebe rubbed her eyes and shook her head to remove the scary vision. A breeze ruffled the surface of the stream, and the image and the feeling faded. Then she heard Grandma's footsteps behind her.

Phoebe turned, looking miserable.

Grandma sighed. "Phoebe, I think we should both apologize to each other."

Phoebe knew Grandma was right. But she wasn't sure what to say, so stood shuffling.

"I wanted you to meet my friends because I'm so proud of you," Grandma continued. "I thought we would all enjoy a lunch together."

"We don't eat like that at home," Phoebe

whispered. "I didn't know what to do …
I'm sorry."

Grandma hugged her. "So am I. I shouldn't
have tried to show you off." She patted
Phoebe's shoulder. "I'm sorry you found
it embarrassing. Would you like to slip
upstairs with a plate of nibbles and look
at the family photo album, while I finish
lunch with my friends?"

Phoebe gave her a hug of relief and
they went inside. Phoebe ran upstairs and
settled on her bed with the big leather
book.

She loved looking at pictures of Dad
when he was little. His photos showed
loads of golden curls instead of brown
hair, but she always recognized the dimple
in his chin, even in his school photos
when he wore exactly the same uniform
as everyone else. Her favourite photo was
one where he was standing beside an
old-fashioned Gypsy caravan. He was leaning
against the horse's neck and laughing.

The caravan looked like the drawing

of Mr. Toad's caravan in *Wind in the Willows*. "Did you travel with the caravan like Toad, Dad?" Phoebe softly asked the photo. "Or did you go to a Gypsy wedding with dancing and fiddling, like in a fairy tale?" She gazed at the photo for a long time.

That's when something strange happened again. The surface of the photo clouded and changed.

Instead of one child there were two children — the fair-haired boy and a dark tousle-headed girl the same age. Laughing and giggling they unharnessed the horse and led it from the caravan shafts. The boy boosted the girl up on the horse's bare back and leapt up behind her. They galloped off across the field.

Phoebe blinked and shook her head. There was the photo just as it usually was. Just her dad. No girl. She closed the album quickly. She'd always had a good imagination, but this was more than daydreaming — she was seeing things again!

Grandma's friends' voices wafted up the stairs, calling goodbye.

Phoebe leaned over the stairs and waved. "Bye, nice to meet you," she said politely, then went back into her room and rolled her eyes at the mirror.

Grandma began clattering dishes in the kitchen sink. Phoebe went down, picked up the towel, and helped dry. "Grandma, how did Dad get to know Gypsies?"

Grandma snorted. "It was none of my doing."

Phoebe waited.

"They came to the village every summer and camped on the Common, the big field at the top end ... scruffy looking people with horrid dogs. They knocked on cottage doors, selling wooden clothes pegs and telling fortunes." Grandma snorted again. "Fortunes indeed. What rubbish! I had nothing to do with them — didn't even open the door to them — but I couldn't keep your dad away. He struck up a friendship with one of the children and kept sneaking off to play."

"Do Gypsies still come around?"

"I've seen occasional travelling families in the area," Grandma answered, "but they've not visited the village for years. The villagers decided Gypsies weren't welcome any more and chased them off. However, when you've finished drying these pots, you can walk through the village to see the Common where your father's photo was taken." She laughed. "The village is tiny, you won't get lost."

Chapter 3

Grandma and Phoebe walked down the garden to the stream and took the path along its bank.

"Cross this bridge," Grandma pointed. "Follow the path on the other side and you'll come out between two cottages on High Street. Then turn left. The Common is just beyond the village, across the road, after the duck pond. It's perfectly safe to explore. Just stay in sight of the village."

Phoebe nodded and crossed the bridge.

She loved being able to take walks on her own. Now that was something she couldn't do back home in Vancouver.

The bridge was a few old planks and a little wobbly. Phoebe paused in the middle and hesitantly stared into the water. The last two visions had occurred when she was staring at something, but this time nothing strange happened to her reflection. Two little ducklings scuttered out and cheeped at her. She felt in her pockets but couldn't find any snacks, only loose change.

"Next time I'll bring bread," she promised, as the ducklings continued to swim hopefully alongside her until the path turned away.

Phoebe walked under the trailing boughs of weeping willows growing along the stream, then brushed her hand across some fragrant blossoms draping a garden wall. The path between the houses was edged by old oaks that met overhead. Exhilarated by a sense of adventure, she ran full tilt through the cool green tunnel.

She felt as though something special was rushing towards her with the sunlight ahead.

After the shaded path, High Street was eye-squintingly bright. Phoebe halted to give her eyes time to adjust. She was near the Post Office and, remembering the change in her pocket, went in to buy some candy.

"Ah, you're Phoebe Hiller," said the woman behind the counter. "Your grandmother told me you were staying with her." Then she leaned back and called through a door behind her, "Bessie's granddaughter's here."

Oh, not again! Phoebe could feel her face going red and wished the ground would open and swallow her. Two elderly women poked their heads out to look.

"You've got your father's chin," said the first.

"Have you got an accent? Let's hear it then," cackled the second.

"Er, hi," replied Phoebe, then embarrassment took over and she couldn't say a thing.

"Isn't that sweet," said the first woman. "So American."

"Don't mind them," said the postmistress. "They don't get a chance to see many foreigners."

That did it. Phoebe turned and fled. Why couldn't people understand she wasn't a foreigner, just a regular kid from Vancouver?

Phoebe jogged steadily along the village street, eyes straight ahead, looking at no one. She didn't slow down until well past the pub, the church, and the small row of thatched cottages around the village pond. Then she slowed ... came to a full stop ... and stared.

In front of her stretched the Common, a large triangular grassy field, with trees edging the stream on one side, and a hedge along another. Parked in the middle was a vivid green, old-fashioned Gypsy caravan.

Phoebe leaned against a tree to catch her breath, blinked hard, and rubbed her eyes. Was she seeing things again?

The green caravan was still there. So was a piebald horse peacefully eating the grass, and a rumpled-looking dog tied with a rope to the spokes of one of the bright yellow wheels.

Phoebe dropped to the grass beneath the tree, edged around the trunk, and put the small holly bush growing at its base between her and the encampment. Half hidden, she peeped through the branches. Am I going nuts or what? she asked herself. She checked again. A green caravan, with bright yellow trim and wheels, an elaborately painted door, and red steps and shaft.

Yup. This wasn't just any old Gypsy caravan.

This was identical to the one in Grandma's photo album, the one behind her dad.

Chapter 4

Phoebe leaned against the tree trunk. Strange things seemed to be happening. She felt as though a part of her mind was out of control. She carefully examined her feelings. No, she wasn't actually scared, more excited and curious.

She turned and peeked through the holly branches again. The caravan seemed real enough, so did the horse and the dog. Then the door opened and, to Phoebe's surprise, down the steps came Fiona carrying

a small paper bag.

"Cheerio, Mrs. Smith, and thanks for making Mum's clothes pegs," Fiona called, then she skipped off towards the village.

Phoebe glimpsed a dark-haired Gypsy woman waving to Fiona before she disappeared inside the caravan again. A moment later the woman reappeared, edging backwards down the red steps, carrying a potted plant in her hand. She placed it on the top step, then stepped down to the grass and stood back to admire the effect. The dog's tail stirred, and the horse turned and whinnied. The woman shook her finger at it.

"Leave it alone, Daisy," she called in a soft sing-song voice. "There's plenty of fresh grass for you."

Then she turned and looked directly at Phoebe's bush. "Come on out," she said. "I don't bite, though I don't like being spied on."

Phoebe scrambled to her feet in confusion. "No, no … I'm not really spying … " Phoebe stopped. What was she doing? "I'm sorry

... I didn't expect ... I didn't know real Gypsies still camped here."

"We don't usually. Our regular stop is Coney's Meadow, down the road aways." The woman climbed back up a couple of steps and reached inside the caravan to pull out a board that she leaned against a wheel.

Fortune Telling, it proclaimed in large letters, Palm Reading and Crystal Ball. Then in smaller letters, Clothes Pegs and Knife Sharpening.

The Gypsy turned and smiled at Phoebe. "Do you want your fortune told?"

Phoebe shook her head vigorously. "No thanks," she said and turned to go.

"Wait." The Gypsy walked over to Phoebe, gently tilted her chin, and looked at her face. "I think you should," she said softly. "I think you're the one I've been waiting for. What's your name?"

"Phoebe," she stammered. "Phoebe Hiller."

The woman threw her head back and chuckled. Her dark curls bounced in delight and her teeth shone white against her dark skin. "Of course it's Phoebe — what else would it be?"

Phoebe looked at her in total astonishment.

Still chuckling, the Gypsy stuck out her hand. "Delighted to meet you, Phoebe Hiller. I'm Mrs. Smith." She paused. "Mrs. Phoebe Smith."

Now it was Phoebe's turn to stare. "Really? You're called Phoebe?"

Mrs. Smith nodded and walked back to the caravan. "Yes. It's an old Romany name that's been in my family for generations." She gestured inside the doorway to a little painted stool. "Come and sit down, young Phoebe, and let me take a peek at that palm of yours."

Phoebe fiddled in her pocket and brought out her change. "That's all the money I have. Is it enough?"

"This fortune's for love, young Phoebe — for my namesake."

Mrs. Smith sat on the caravan steps,

pulled down the stool, and patted it invitingly. Phoebe perched on it and held out her hand. Mrs. Smith stroked it gently, and as Phoebe's fingers uncurled she ran one finger down the middle of Phoebe's palm. "Nice strong life line," she said, "just as it should be at your age. Now tell me what country is it you live in? I get a feeling of trees ... big trees ... far taller than our English ones ... and lots of water."

"Canada," said Phoebe nodding. "There's lots of trees ... and water. We live by the coast and it rains a lot." Phoebe looked down at her palm then back at the Gypsy. "Could you tell all that from my hand?"

Mrs. Smith pointed to some tiny lines. "These mean you've travelled over water." She chuckled, "And your accent isn't English, so you must have come here from another country."

Phoebe laughed with delight. "So it's not all magic then. You guessed when I talked to you."

The Gypsy smiled and took Phoebe's palm again.

"Way in the future you will marry and have two children, but you are probably not worried about that now?"

Phoebe grinned and shook her head.

"Hmm … Looks like his name will start with R … the name Rob comes to me."

"Rob!" Phoebe shrieked and pulled her hand back and stared at it. "Rob Kyle? No way. I hate him."

Mrs. Smith chuckled and reached out again for Phoebe's hand. "There may be more than one Rob in your life."

"You bet there will," Phoebe muttered.

The Gypsy looked down again. "I see a new dress … one that's important to you … a special occasion. Are you going to a wedding?"

Phoebe stared in astonishment. "Yes. That's why we've come to England. Uncle Gerald is getting married in two weeks and I'm to be a bridesmaid … but I haven't seen the dress yet. I try it on next week."

Mrs. Smith patted her knee. "Well, stop worrying about it. You'll look a sight for sore eyes."

Wow ... now that was impressive. Phoebe wondered how Mrs. Smith could tell she'd been scared of looking like a freak.

"But I see a spot of trouble in your life, something involving water."

Phoebe's eyes widened. "Sounds scary."

"Not necessarily, but let's take a look." Mrs. Smith reached in her skirt pocket and drew out a black velvet bag. She pulled the drawstring top and tipped out a small crystal ball. "Cradle this in your hands for a few minutes, Phoebe, then hold it up so I can look inside."

The crystal felt cold to the touch, and no matter how long Phoebe warmed it between her palms, it stayed cold. Eventually she gave up and held the crystal towards Mrs. Smith, who gazed in it intently.

"Yes ... trouble with water will come to you soon. It will frighten you, but don't worry ... you'll be fine if you'll watch for the dog … a dog … and something red."

Phoebe frowned. "I don't like dogs. One bit me when I was little." She pointed to her calf. "I've still got scars. I don't understand how a dog could help."

Mrs. Smith smiled gently. "Neither do I. I can only tell what I see in the crystal, and it doesn't always make sense until it happens. Do you want to look?"

Phoebe wasn't sure, but curiosity won. She nodded. Mrs. Smith held the crystal up to her eye level.

At first there was nothing to see, just the sunshine reflected off a cloudy glass ball. Phoebe stared and stared, and just as she was about to give up, the mistiness inside stirred like smoke … and the smoke parted.

Two small figures came running towards her. The boy with the golden curls stretched out his hand and grabbed the Gypsy girl's hand to drag her along faster. Her long dark curls were streaming in the wind and she was laughing at him with white teeth that gleamed against her dusky skin.

There was something familiar in the smile and the way the child tossed her hair. Phoebe's eyes flew from the crystal to Mrs. Smith's face.

"It's ... it's you ... you as a child ... you and my dad .... You're the Gypsy kid he played with!"

Mrs. Smith nodded and lowered the crystal.

"And you're his daughter. And you've got 'the sight' like he had."

Chapter 5

Stunned, Phoebe sat with a hundred and one questions whirling around her brain. There was so much she wanted to ask that she didn't know where to start. She looked at Mrs. Smith with wondering eyes.

"I ... I keep seeing things," she stammered. "Things that aren't really there. Is that having 'the sight,' like Gypsies? I thought I was just daydreaming!"

Mrs. Smith nodded. "Lots of people see things, but most choose to ignore them."

"Dad's never said anything," said Phoebe uncertainly.

Mrs. Smith nodded sadly. "I know. His mother is uncomfortable with Gypsies. She sometimes prevented him from playing with me. Your father didn't speak about our friendship and he was afraid to admit he had the gift."

"But Dad's not a Gypsy. Neither am I."

"Lots of people have the gift, not just Romany people. It's just that we hone our gift — polish it and use it — but Gorgios fear it."

"Does ... er, Gorgios ... mean me?" asked Phoebe, stumbling over the unfamiliar word.

"Yes, anyone who isn't a Romany."

"What's a Romany?"

Mrs. Smith laughed. "We're a race of people without a homeland but with our own language, customs, and travelling way of life. Some folk say we originally came from India a thousand years ago. Romanies are found in many countries.

My family has relatives in Greece, Yugoslavia, and Russia, but we've lived in England for several hundred years, mostly around the New Forest." She patted the steps of the caravan. "These traditional wagons are handed down through families for generations. We live in them and move from village to village telling fortunes, making and selling clothes pegs, sharpening knives and doing odd jobs for people." She gestured towards the village. "Some people watch for us. Fiona's mother buys pegs from me every year. And the farm over at Swithin's Dell hires us each spring to help with the lambing."

Phoebe had so many questions. But one question kept running around and around and getting so big, she was almost too scared to ask about it. She thought of her dad and mom. Then her brain replayed the vision of her dad and the Gypsy child laughing and running through the fields, hand in hand. Her eyes brimmed with tears.

"Why Phoebe, don't cry. You have an unusual talent ... it's nothing to be afraid of."

Phoebe shook her head. "No, it's not that," she gulped. "It's just — " She couldn't stop it. A tear escaped and trickled down beside her nose. She brushed it away angrily. "Does that mean my dad doesn't love my mom? That he loves you ... and that's why I'm called Phoebe?"

Two arms gently hugged her and a cloud of dark hair scented with lavender and a hint of wood smoke brushed comfortingly against her face.

"No, no," whispered Mrs. Smith. "It wasn't like that. I was your dad's best friend when he was young. We only saw each other in the summer holidays — for two short weeks each year — until we were twelve years old."

She leaned back and looked into Phoebe's eyes. "The Romany and Gorgio ways are very different, but some of us become good friends. Your dad always said he would never forget our friendship." She gave Phoebe a little squeeze. "And he didn't. You're my namesake, a childhood memory, and a compliment!"

Phoebe blew her nose and gathered enough courage to ask the next question. "What did you mean when you said you'd been waiting for me?"

Mrs. Smith stood up and stretched like a cat in the sunshine. The dog crawled out from under the caravan and pawed at her leg. She bent down and scratched its ears absentmindedly.

Phoebe edged away nervously.

"I'm not sure why I'm here," Mrs. Smith replied. "We've not camped on this common for years. In the past, the village was unfriendly."

Phoebe stretched out a cramped leg and the dog's head turned. It looked up at her and growled softly, its fur bristling. Phoebe gasped and leaned back, almost falling off the stool.

Mrs. Smith shot out her arm and tightened

the dog's rope. "Now then, Bendigo. I know you're a Gypsy guard dog, but Phoebe's a friend."

Phoebe hurriedly pulled her leg back out of reach. The dog subsided and leaned against Mrs. Smith.

"I had an urge, a feeling I should visit here again. So I looked in the crystal and saw you," Mrs. Smith hesitated. "I have no idea why. Maybe I can help you in some way ... answer your questions — or maybe it's for some other reason. Time will tell." She looked up at the sun. "The afternoon's moving on and I have a couple of customers coming for readings. Why don't you come back tomorrow? I'll show you some of the things I showed your dad."

"O.K. I'll come if I can." Phoebe turned to go, then halted in surprise.

"Good afternoon, Phoebe," said Miss Abbots as she picked her way gingerly across the daisy-sprinkled grass. "I see you've met Mrs. Smith." She lifted her finger to her lips and dropped her voice. "But I won't tell your grandma about you, if you don't tell her about me," and to Phoebe's astonishment, staid Miss Abbots actually winked.

Wow, thought Phoebe, so Miss Abbots knows Grandma doesn't approve of Gypsies and fortune telling. She turned and watched the two women greet each other like old friends and climb into the caravan.

Phoebe walked home thoughtfully. "Perhaps I'd better not mention Mrs. Smith. I don't want Grandma saying I can't come back tomorrow."

Chapter 6

The following day was bright and polished, with a sky as shiny blue as Grandma's favourite china bowl. Phoebe helped Grandma mow the lawn and pick some early strawberries for lunch.

"What do you want to do this afternoon?" asked Grandma as they sprinkled sugar over the berries, poured cream on the top, and slowly savoured every mouthful.

Phoebe tried to sound casual. "Can I feed the ducks and explore again?"

"There's not much to see. I could take you for a drive somewhere else if you liked," Grandma added, worried.

"I like it here."

Grandma looked pleased. "Fine." She found some crusts of bread and gave them to Phoebe in a plastic bag. "I'll do more gardening while the weather's nice. Just remember to — "

"Stay within sight of the village," chanted Phoebe along with her.

Mrs. Smith was grooming Daisy when Phoebe breathlessly arrived. She handed Phoebe the brush and showed her how to slip the strap over her hand so the brush fitted comfortably into her palm. "Brush with long firm strokes, in the same way as her coat lies."

Phoebe brushed the glossy coat and watched the way Daisy half closed her eyes and leaned into the strokes. "She loves it."

"Of course. Horses are like people — they enjoy affection."

Mrs. Smith gently slapped Daisy's rump, then bent down and lifted a back hoof and scraped out the dirt.

"Can I see?" Phoebe came around to watch. "How are the horseshoes attached?"

Mrs. Smith pointed out the nails through Daisy's hoof. "Do you have a lucky horse-shoe?"

Phoebe shook her head.

"I'll see if I can find an old one for you. If you nail one over your door, curve down and points up, your luck will never run out." She moved around the horse and finished the hooves, then straightened up.

"So, young Phoebe, would you like to see how the Romany people live?"

"I promised Grandma I'd stay in sight of the village."

"Then we will."

Mrs. Smith showed Phoebe how to explore the secrets hidden around the Common, and the afternoon wrapped them in a golden bubble of sunlight.

"It's not just an empty field any more," said Phoebe in fascination as they fetched water from the stream and gathered dead oak branches for a campfire. "It's a home."

Mrs. Smith nodded and showed Phoebe how to stack the wood deep in the hedge to keep dry.

"Hey, there's some wood already stacked," Phoebe pointed.

"Yes, another Romany has passed by," said Mrs. Smith. "We always leave some ready for the next traveller. We'll burn their dry wood and leave ours."

"Now use my knife," instructed Mrs. Smith, "cut down into the turf, make a large square, then we'll carefully slit underneath it."

Together they lifted the turf and put it on one side. Mrs. Smith showed Phoebe how to build a safe campfire in its hollow. She placed a small iron tripod over the flames and hung a billy-can of water to heat.

"Can you see my grocery store?" asked Mrs. Smith, and she pointed out the wild herbs growing along the hedgerow.

Phoebe picked chamomile and sweet cicely and, lifting the bunches to her nose, took a deep sniff. "I wonder why people don't make perfume from these," she said appreciatively.

Mrs. Smith smiled and threw the herbs in the billy-can along with sprigs of lavender snipped from the pot on her windowsill. The water boiled, sending up wisps of fragrant steam. She stirred it, then poured out two cups of the herbal tea. The remainder she poured in a glass jar, screwed the lid on tight, and set it on the caravan steps.

"You can take this home and use it to rinse your hair next time you wash it."

"Will it make my hair smell like yours?" Phoebe asked, delighted. Mrs. Smith nodded.

"Can you show me something else you and Dad did?" Phoebe requested after she'd drained her cup.

She and Mrs. Smith took off their shoes and walked over to the stream. Mrs. Smith hoisted up her skirt and paddled to gather watercress. Phoebe rolled up the legs of her jeans and jumped in to help.

"Look." Mrs. Smith held out her palm to show Phoebe some caddis fly larvae. They were encased in beautiful mosaic crusts made of tiny pebbles, shells, and fragments of glass.

"The larvae glue together whatever they can find from the stream bottom," she explained. "They make protective cases for their soft bodies." She waited patiently while Phoebe searched until she found an empty one to keep.

Suddenly Mrs. Smith pointed silently. She'd spotted a hole in the opposite bank. They sat, dangling their feet in the water, and quietly watched. To Phoebe's delight, a kingfisher darted out.

"Listen," whispered Mrs. Smith, and the afternoon was so still they could hear a faint calling from within the bank. Phoebe froze, scarcely daring to breathe. They were rewarded by seeing the kingfisher dart in and out several times. It carried small fish to feed the young birds.

Further along, just before the stream slipped lazily into the village pond, they stretched out together under a tree and gazed into a shadowy pool where the trout lay resting. Mrs. Smith snaked one arm slowly into the water without causing a ripple and "tickled" the trout's belly until — FLIP. With one movement it was up on the bank, gasping. She wrapped it in leaves to carry it back for her supper.

"I'd better go now," said Phoebe as she walked barefoot across the Common to the caravan. "Grandma will be getting tea ready."

"I'm glad I met you, young Phoebe."

"Me too." Phoebe threw her arms around Mrs. Smith's waist and hugged with all her might. "I'm proud I've got your name. I'll never forget you." She slipped on her sandals and picked up her jar of tea. Carefully avoiding Bendigo, she patted Daisy for the last time and ran towards the village street, her head filled with wonders.

Chapter 7

Beyond the pond Phoebe paused. In the distance she could see the two old ladies from the Post Office. "Oh no," she groaned. "I'll have to pass them to get to the short cut. They'll want me to talk to them again." She swiftly dodged away and turned down Acorn Lane to Grandma's house.

"I'm home," Phoebe called as she ran upstairs and placed her jar of tea on the dresser. No one answered, and the house had a flat, echoey feeling. She wandered back downstairs to the living room and kitchen, but both were empty.

I wonder if Grandma's still gardening? she thought.

Phoebe opened the back door and stepped out into the garden. "Grandma?"

No one answered. Phoebe began to feel uneasy. She walked down the garden towards the stream. "Grandma, where are you?"

A faint moan drifted through the air.

Frightened, Phoebe ran towards the bridge. Then she froze in horror. Grandma was lying on her back in the stream, with a gash on her forehead. Strands of her white hair were waving in the current, and ripples of water were washing almost over her face.

"Grandma — what happened?" Phoebe leaped into the water and cradled Grandma's head and shoulders. "Grandma — talk to me."

Grandma moaned and tried to raise

one hand towards her forehead, but it flopped back and her eyes closed. Blood seeped down the side of her face and dripped on Phoebe's jeans.

"HELP!" called Phoebe at the top of her lungs, and she struggled to drag Grandma out of the water. "PLEASE — someone HELP!"

Phoebe's feet slipped in the mud and she sat down hard in the water with Grandma's body on top of her. Grandma groaned again.

Terrified, Phoebe tried to remember the first-aid classes she'd taken for babysitting, but she couldn't think straight.

She patted Grandma's cheek. "Wake up Grandma … Please wake up … don't die."

Grandma's head lolled against Phoebe's shoulder, her face chalky white. Her body was so heavy that Phoebe couldn't drag her towards the low bank. Phoebe sat in the cold stream with her arms around Grandma's chest, lifting her head and shoulders clear of the water.

"HEEELLP!" Phoebe hollered again at the top of her voice. "Please someone … HEEELLP!"

Barking excitedly, a large black dog burst through the willows and stood on the bank, panting and slobbering.

Phoebe shrank back as far as she could. "No, go away," she said desperately. "You're not the help I need. Go AWAY!"

The dog stood his ground and barked again, showing shiny white fangs.

Appalled, Phoebe glared back at it. That's when she noticed a slash of red around the dog's neck, and heard Mrs. Smith's voice in her head.

Trouble with water will come to you soon. It will frighten you, but don't worry … you'll be fine if you'll watch for the dog … a dog … and something red.

And there it was, a shiny new red leather collar buckled around the dog's neck.

Phoebe gazed at the dog in horror.

Did this mean she was going to have to touch it? What if it bit her?

"Are you a friendly dog?" asked Phoebe fearfully.

The dog looked at her, ears cocked, head on one side, and its tail waved slowly.

Phoebe looked at the dog and back at Grandma and knew this was her only chance. She screwed up her courage and clicked her tongue tentatively. "Here boy ... come on ... here."

The dog looked interested but made no move off the bank.

Phoebe tried again. "Here ... come on dog ... I need you to help me."

The dog barked once.

Phoebe began to cry angrily. "OK, do it your way," she sobbed. "At least you could bark as I shout. HELP! HELP!"

Phoebe hollered, Grandma stirred in her arms and moaned, but the dog just wagged its tail furiously.

Frantically, Phoebe looked around. Grandma's bag was wedged in the reeds by the bank. She heaved Grandma to one side so she could support her with one arm. Then she leaned sideways and grabbed the bag's handle, flicked open the clasp, and tipped out the contents on top of Grandma. Several things rolled into the water, but she managed to grab a clean hanky and a lipstick.

Phoebe spread the hanky over the bag's plastic surface, pulled the top of the lipstick off with her teeth, and wrote HELP MRS. HILLERS HOUSE in big red letters. It was smudgy, but legible.

Then she tentatively called the dog again. "Come on boy … I need you. Come on … here boy … here, so I can pat you." Phoebe cajoled and sweet-talked for what seemed like ages, until finally her anger and desperation overcame her fear.

"COME HERE!" she roared with authority.

At last the dog stepped off the bank, paddled over to them, and swept a long red tongue over Phoebe's face. Phoebe

cringed but made herself grab the dog's collar.

Her hands shook and fumbled, but she managed to tie one corner of the hanky firmly around the red leather strap.

Despite her terror, Phoebe struggled to appear confident. "Listen, Swamp Breath, go and find your owner. GO HOME!" She balled her fist, closed her eyes, and swung her arm to thump his backside. The dog leaped up the bank with a yelp and shot into the bushes. Phoebe shuddered with relief.

The waiting was awful. What if the dog wouldn't go to someone? What if people didn't understand the message?

Well, she couldn't just sit there waiting. Phoebe used the hem of her shirt to wipe the blood off Grandma's face, then she tied a smooth pebble in it and gently pressed it against the gash on Grandma's head to stanch the bleeding.

"HELP. HEEEELLP."

What if Grandma really died?

Phoebe couldn't let herself think any more. She sat blankly in the stream getting colder and colder. She couldn't leave, for the vision of Grandma's face slipping under the water was etched in her mind, and Phoebe knew Grandma would drown before she arrived back with help.

Phoebe shouted with renewed vigour. Finally she heard the dog barking again, and voices. The postmistress and a man Phoebe had not seen before hurtled over the bridge.

"Lordy, Lordy, what a thing to happen!" cried the postmistress. She and the man stepped into the stream and gently lifted Grandma off Phoebe and onto the bank.

"I'll ph-ph-phone the doctor," Phoebe blubbered with relief as she scrambled out of the stream and ran up to the house, shirt flapping and sandals squelching.

Chapter 8

Within minutes the local doctor and a nurse arrived, followed closely by an ambulance that whisked Grandma off to the hospital.

"Your granny is in good hands," the nurse said. "Now we have to stop you getting pneumonia." And she shooed Phoebe back into the house and hustled her upstairs to the bathroom.

Phoebe's numb fingers fumbled over the shirt buttons. The nurse helped her.

"I've run a hot bath for you, now sit and soak until you stop shivering."

The bath was deep and old-fashioned and the water steaming hot. The nurse poured in some green bath salts from a glass jar on the window sill. "I gave these to Bessie years ago. She's never used them, so why don't you enjoy them?"

Phoebe smiled shakily, and gingerly lowered herself into the fragrant water. She lay back thankfully and let the chills and tension begin to soak out of her body. It had been quite a day.

It was an hour before Phoebe returned to the kitchen wearing her PJs and swathed in Grandma's velvet housecoat. She gazed in astonishment. The kitchen was full of neighbours, and everyone had brought food! Cakes, casseroles, and cookies, loaves of bread, and an assortment of pies covered every available surface.

"Grandma won't have to cook for weeks,"

she said in wonder.

"That's the idea," said the nurse, pulling out a chair for Phoebe. "The villagers always rally round in times of trouble."

Phoebe sat at the table sipping a gigantic mug of steaming cocoa and looking at everyone. "How's Grandma?"

"She's fine and she's conscious," Dr. Pratt reassured her. "But we need to make sure the bump on her head won't give her concussion and that she's not caught a chill from lying in the cold water."

"Do you know what happened?" Phoebe asked.

"She tripped on the bridge and hit her head as she fell," he explained.

"I always said that bridge was unsafe, needs a handrail," muttered Mrs. Andrews the postmistress. "Maybe someone will do something now."

Several neighbours nodded in agreement.

"Thank goodness you went to look for her, Phoebe. And sending the dog like that

— who would have thought of that now?" Mrs. Andrews patted Phoebe on the shoulder, and someone else said, "Good job."

Phoebe's eyes filled with tears. "Was it my fault she fell? Was she looking for me?"

"Heavens no," said Mrs. Andrews. "I'd just phoned her to say the grocery order was in. She was coming to pick it up. You arrived home just as it happened. You saved her life."

Phoebe smiled with relief and blew her nose hard.

Mrs. Andrews patted her again. "Now don't you worry, young Phoebe. Your gran will be fine and home in a few days."

The doctor nodded in agreement. "Could be sooner if there are no problems." He smiled. "Bessie's a tough old bird."

"Our Kathy will stay with you until your mum and dad get back," Mrs. Andrews continued.

Kathy Andrews grinned across at Phoebe She looked about eighteen, with spiky dark hair and a stud in the side of her nose.

"Cool," said Phoebe and grinned shakily back.

It was ages before everyone left. They were incredibly kind, but Phoebe felt overwhelmed by the strange faces and everyone talking at once. She was glad to see them go, but remembered to thank them all, especially the dog's owner. He turned out to be a young farmer called Peter Bainbridge.

"My dog's not the brightest animal. He doesn't always answer to his own name," said Peter Bainbridge, ruffling her hair as he got up to leave. "How on earth did you get him to cooperate?"

"I called him Swamp Breath and thumped his bum," said Phoebe, blushing.

Everyone laughed.

"Pretty appropriate if you ask me," said Mrs. Andrews.

"What's his real name?" Phoebe asked.

"Midnight," said Peter Bainbridge, "but

I've a feeling he might be Swamp Breath from now on."

Finally Kathy Andrews and Phoebe were left on their own. Kathy cooked mashed potatoes, and both girls tucked into generous slices of a cold meat pie someone had brought, along with half a jar of pickles.

It was only 6:30 P.M., but Phoebe couldn't keep her eyes open.

"Why don't you go to bed?" Kathy asked. "You're exhausted after all the fuss." She walked behind Phoebe and lifted up the trailing hem of Grandma's housecoat. Phoebe staggered up the stairs and rolled into bed.

"What about you?" asked Phoebe sleepily.

Kathy grinned. "I'll watch TV — all the rock video shows my mum hates — and wait for your parents."

Phoebe nodded drowsily. Kathy closed the curtains and tiptoed out.

Chapter 9

Phoebe sat up with a start. She didn't usually have nightmares, but this one was still vivid, making her heart race.

The room was dark and she leaned back against the pillows. Then her eyelids drooped again and the dream images came flooding back.

She was floating in the air, flying at great speed, swooping over fields and woods and hills and lakes. Her hair streamed

behind her and she was laughing. Eventually she glimpsed the village and slowed, circling lower and lower until she hovered above. The village spread below.

Several Gypsy caravans were parked in a circle on the Common. Children were playing, and among them were the golden-haired boy and the tousle-haired Gypsy girl.

Suddenly they left the group, running off to explore the stream. They wandered along the bank until they found themselves in a wooded area where the stream ran deep and fast. A large willow overhung a small weir. Both children climbed the tree and swung out on a large branch, laughing and chattering, their feet dangling over the water.

With a sudden SNAP, the willow branch broke, tumbling the children into the water.

"The weir," gasped Phoebe, waking suddenly but still feeling the terror. Her body was sticky with sweat. "The children were swept over the weir."

Kathy knocked on the door and crept in to switch on a lamp.

"You OK?" she asked, perching on the bed. "I thought I heard you call."

"It was a dream; it woke me."

"Probably a nightmare," Kathy said practically. "You went through a lot this afternoon."

"What's the time?" Phoebe asked groggily.

"Eight o'clock. Your parents say they'll be here by nine."

Phoebe nodded and settled down again. Kathy tiptoed out.

Soaked and shaken, the two children huddled on a small beach against a steep bank. Again and again they tried to scramble up, but the sides crumbled away. Eventually the boy helped the girl climb on his shoulders so she could reach some overhanging roots above their heads. She pulled herself up, then lay down and pulled him up.

Exhausted, they lay for a long time regaining their strength.

It was dark before they stumbled back to the village. Filthy, still damp, and almost unrecognizable, they crossed the Common, only to meet an angry crowd of villagers.

The boy was snatched from the girl's side.

"What have them Gyppos done to you? ... Tell us ... we'll kill 'em."

The boy shook his head. "Nothing ... no one's done anything." He turned to look for the girl, but she'd melted away into the night.

"Always knew them thieving Gypsies would cause trouble," said a voice.

There was a rumble of agreement.

"Did they try to kidnap you?" demanded someone else.

"No ... no," said the boy wearily. "We were playing ... we fell in the river ... I just want to go home."

"You were with that Gypsy brat," said a man, and gave the boy a clip over the ear. "That'll larn you to mess with them."

The scene grew smaller and smaller. Phoebe flew away again, away from the anger, away from the fear. Her body's feeling of exhaustion faded, and she relaxed. She turned on the pillow, cupped her hand under her cheek, breathed softly and evenly, and dreamed no more.

Chapter 10

She woke to the smell of bacon and the rise and fall of morning voices in the kitchen. Running downstairs, Phoebe found not only her parents but Grandma.

"Yay! You're back." She threw herself on Grandma and almost squeezed her to death, then ran round the table hugging everyone else, several times over.

"Steady, steady," said Grandma. "Don't knock me over."

"I thought you were going to be in

hospital for days?"

Grandma snorted. "What? For a bump on the head? Not me. I told Dr. Pratt I wasn't staying. Hospitals are no place for people to get well — too many sick folk. All I need is a bit of peace and quiet." She glared at Phoebe and her parents. They all laughed.

Grandma rested while Phoebe's mom and dad organized a roster of neighbours to come in each day and clean and help with the cooking for a couple of weeks.

"All I want is to be left alone," Grandma grumbled. But each time a neighbour dropped in to tease her and exchange the latest village gossip, more colour flooded her cheeks and she seemed a little stronger.

People also came to see Phoebe. They said nice things, telling her parents how clever she'd been in sending the dog to get help.

Even Fiona from next door came. "My

mum says you're a hero," she said, looking at Phoebe with admiration. "Want to come and see my rabbit?"

Phoebe felt proud but embarrassed. I'm not a hero, she thought. I would never have thought of using the dog without Mrs. Smith. I must go to the Common and tell her what happened, and ask her about the dream.

Phoebe looked across at Grandma and wondered if she dared explain about the Gypsy. She tried to catch her father on his own, but visits from the neighbours or the doctor interrupted them.

With all the fuss, it was midafternoon before Phoebe could slip away. She ran swiftly up Acorn Lane and over the bridge.

The Common was empty.

Phoebe felt as though she'd been hit in the stomach.

"Not fair!" she yelled and kicked a small rock. "I need Phoebe Smith. I need to ask about the dreams and if they really happened. I want to bring my dad … " She stopped and looked sadly around the empty patch of land. "But what if everything was in my imagination?" she whispered sadly.

She stomped around, kicking daisy heads.

There was almost nothing to show a Gypsy had camped there. The turf, carefully replaced, hid the spot where they'd built the fire and brewed tea. The scattered horse droppings could have been evidence of one of the local horses, and the grass was already springing up where it had been flattened by the wagon wheels. Had her wonderful afternoon really happened?

She walked over to the hedge. Neatly tucked inside was a stash of dry wood, safely hidden for the next traveller — but it too looked as though it had been lying there for ages.

At the base of the hedge was a dark shape. Phoebe pushed her arm through the branches and pulled it out.

A horseshoe lay in her hand, a lucky

horseshoe. Phoebe knew it wasn't there yesterday when she stacked the wood.

"Oh, Mrs. Smith," Phoebe whispered, "I wish I could thank you." She threaded the horseshoe carefully through a belt loop on her jeans and headed back to Grandma's house.

Chapter 11

They waved goodbye to Grandma that evening.

Mom and Dad didn't really want to leave, but Grandma insisted they carry on with their holiday. She needed time on her own.

"I'll be fine. I just want to be able to relax in bed, without worrying about guests in the house."

"We'll phone and check in every day," reassured Dad.

"You and the rest of the village," grumbled Grandma with a wry smile.

Grandma gave an extra hug to Phoebe. "I'm so glad you were here to rescue me. I'll look forward to seeing you at the wedding." She tugged playfully at Phoebe's jeans. "It'll be a real treat to see you dressed up to the nines for a change." She touched the discoloured area around her temple and the stitched-up gash. "Thank goodness my bruises will have almost disappeared by then." She laughed. "I'll have to wear a hat with a floppy brim."

Phoebe twisted around on the back seat of the car so she could watch Grandma out of the back window. It's weird knowing you've saved someone's life, she thought as she waved. In a funny way it makes me feel older than her.

They waved and waved at each other until the car turned the corner at the end of Acorn Lane.

As Dad drove past the Common, Phoebe leaned through the gap between the front seats and touched him on the shoulder. "A Gypsy caravan camped there yesterday."

The car immediately slowed down and Dad turned to look. "I knew a Gypsy once," he said slowly. "She was called Phoebe like you, and for a while she was my best friend."

Phoebe opened her mouth to tell him, then noticed her mom had placed a hand on her father's knee and he'd dropped one of his hands from the steering wheel and was holding hers tight. So tightly his knuckles were white. Embarrassed, Phoebe looked back at the Common.

That was when the "seeing thing" happened again.

The caravan was surrounded by people yelling and shouting.

"Get out of here and don't come back, you horse thieves."

"Leave our kids alone."

A swarthy-looking man, face set, finished harnessing the horse and turned to lead it through the crowd. As he moved forward, another chorus of derisive shouts broke out. A tomato flew threw the air, hit his shoulder, burst, and dripped down the arm of his jacket.

Two policemen held the angry crowd back, and the caravan slowly passed through. A small frightened face framed with a cloud of dark curls peeped out of the back window.

"Leave them alone," came a cry. "They've not done anything." The young fair-haired boy tried to break through the crowd and help the Gypsy with the horse.

The policeman grabbed his arm. "Let it be, son, or the village may turn on you. They're best gone."

The boy watched helplessly as the caravan creaked its way across the Common and onto the road.

Phoebe clamped her mouth shut and leaned back against the car seat. If her sightings were true, there was more going on than she'd realized. Something her dad found painful to talk about.

She watched her dad's hand. After they'd passed the Common, his grip gradually relaxed. Her mom patted his knee gently, he replaced both hands on the wheel, and the car picked up speed.

They were at Uncle Gerald's house before Phoebe got a chance to talk to her father on his own. She'd gone to bed to read and he slipped upstairs to tuck her in.

"Dad, can I tell you something ... something that you mustn't tell Grandma?"

Dad nodded and sat on the bed. "What's bothering you, pumpkin. Something to do with the accident?"

Phoebe nodded. "Sort of, Dad. That Gypsy you knew ... Phoebe ... I met her."

A look of utter sadness crossed her father's face. "You can't have, love."

"But Dad, I did. We spent the afternoon together. She showed me all kinds of things … " Phoebe tailed off as her father shook his head.

"You cannot have met the Phoebe I knew," he said. "She died when she was twelve. She caught a chill after falling in the river — "

"Who told you that?" Phoebe interrupted.

Her father looked confused. "I don't remember … there was talk … in the village."

"Then it wasn't true." Phoebe sat up in bed. "Dad, I really did meet her. She's called Mrs. Smith now. We spent the afternoon together. She told my fortune and showed me how to make a campfire. We gathered watercress and she tickled trout."

Her father stared. "She's alive? I've had nightmares for years … I thought it was my fault she caught pneumonia."

Phoebe slipped out of bed, found the jar of tea in her suitcase, and thrust it under her father's nose. "See, she gave me this to rinse my hair. I'm going to use it for the wedding."

Her father unscrewed the lid and sniffed. "Lavender," he said softly and smiled. "I'd forgotten she always smelled faintly of lavender." Then he lay beside Phoebe and listened while she told him the full story.

Her father lay silent for so long after Phoebe finished talking that she sat up and turned her head to look at him. "Are you mad at me?"

Phoebe's father pulled her close. "No, I'm confused, astonished, and sad and happy at the same time. But still very proud of you."

"What about my seeing things? Mrs. Smith said you could do it too."

There was another long pause. "I'm going to tell you something that you must never tell Grandma." Her father looked at her with a faint trace of embarrassment. "When the phone call came about the accident, we were just getting ready to leave early. You see, I had this terrible feeling something was wrong and we needed to get back."

I'm glad I met you, Phoebe Smith, thought Phoebe as she finally settled down to sleep.

The Gypsy's voice drifted into her mind.

I'm not sure why I'm here. We've not been this way for years. Maybe I can help you in some way ... answer your questions ... or it may be for some other reason. Time will tell.

I know why you came, thought Phoebe sleepily, as she slipped her hand under the pillow and gently stroked the horseshoe. It was not just to help me.

You also came to help my dad.

Andrea Spalding is a writer, storyteller, teacher and historical consultant. Her children's books include *The Most Beautiful Kite in the World, Finders Keepers*, and *An Island of My Own*, which was shortlisted for the Silver Birch Award. Her most recent picturebook, *Sarah May and the New Red Dress* (illustrated by Janet Wilson), was nominated for the prestigious Ruth Schwartz Children's Literature Award. It was also selected for the Ontario Library Association's "Best Bets for 1998." Andrea's stories are full of emotion, excitement, humour and love for the Canadian landscape.

Born and raised in England, Andrea and her husband moved to Alberta, where they raised three daughters. In 1990, Andrea and her husband settled in their own bed & breakfast retreat on Pender Island, British Columbia, off Canada's southwest coast.